For Nicholas
L.J.

For Lily Mae,
welcome to the world!
C.W.

Text copyright © 1995 by Linda Jennings
Illustrations copyright © 1995 by Catherine Walters
All rights reserved.
CIP Data is available.
First published in the United States 1995 by
Dutton Children's Books,
a division of Penguin Books USA Inc.
375 Hudson Street, New York, New York 10014
Originally published in Great Britain 1995 by
Magi Publications, London
Typography by Carolyn Boschi
Printed in Belgium
First American Edition
ISBN 0-525-45364-4
1 3 5 7 9 10 8 6 4 2

THE
Brave Little Bunny

by **Linda Jennings**
illustrated by **Catherine Walters**

DUTTON CHILDREN'S BOOKS
New York

Millie was a lop-eared rabbit who lived with her sisters and brother in a small backyard hutch.

Millie had loved their cozy home when she was a little bunny, but now that she was almost a grown rabbit, the hutch seemed small and cramped. Millie was tired of eating the same old lettuce and carrots every day and of not having enough space to hop in.

Staring out through the wire mesh of the hutch, Millie could see a tall hedge at the end of the yard. She longed to see what was on the other side of those bushes.

One warm spring evening, somebody left the door to the hutch open. Millie knew this was her chance. She said good-bye to her family and, with a flick of her white tail, scampered across the yard to the hedge. She burrowed underneath it and came out on the other side...

…where a fox was waiting for her! Millie froze. The fox took a step forward....Then Millie heard the thumping of rabbit feet and an excited voice call out, "Run! Run this way!"

She turned and bolted toward the sound.

"In here," ordered the same voice, and Millie shot into a small hole in the ground.

The fox tried to follow but could not fit through the entrance to the burrow.

"That was close," said a large gray rabbit with ears that stuck straight up.

"Yes," gasped Millie.

"Why didn't you run?" asked the strange rabbit. He sniffed Millie curiously.

"I've never had to before. Foxes can't get into my hutch," she replied.

"Oh! You're a pet rabbit," he said a bit disdainfully. "I wondered what was wrong with your ears, but I guess they're supposed to look that way."

The fox had gone, so the two rabbits came up into the field again.

"My name is Millie."

"I'm Seventy-six," said the wild rabbit.

"Is that a name?" asked Millie, unsure.

"Sort of. There are a lot of rabbits in my family, so we are called by numbers instead of names," Seventy-six explained.

"Oh," said Millie, looking around with interest.

The wild rabbit scampered off. Millie ran after him. The young rabbits chased each other around the meadow. Millie stopped now and then to look at the field mice or to taste the sweet clover and tender green grass.

The sun was gone, and the wide stretch of sky above
the meadow turned a soft pink. Millie began to won-
der where she should go when it got dark.

"You can come stay with my family," suggested her
new friend.

They hopped to the edge of the meadow where the family of wild rabbits was feeding.

"Is that a *pet* rabbit?" asked one.

"What's wrong with her ears?" asked another.

"She can't stay with us," said Father Rabbit. "A rabbit who doesn't have the sense to run away from a fox would be a danger to our warren."

Father Rabbit rose up on his hind legs and thumped the ground threateningly.

He stared down at Millie. "Go back to wherever you came from. You are not welcome here." Then he lunged forward, his teeth bared.

Millie didn't even have time to say good-bye to Seventy-six. She turned and bolted toward the hedge. She burrowed back into her yard and ran to the hutch.

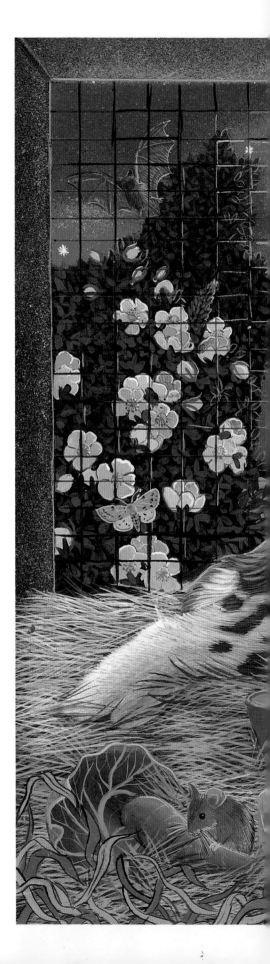

But the door was locked now. Millie would have to wait for someone to come in the morning and let her in.

But the longer she stared at her sleeping family, the more Millie realized she didn't want to be back inside the hutch. What if she never got out again? She wouldn't be able to run or eat clover…or talk to her new friend.

Millie hopped back across the yard. She wasn't sure where she was going. It was very dark.

A shadow moved near the hedge. Was it the fox? Millie stopped. Should she run?

"Millie, it's me—Seventy-six," said the shadow. "I've left the warren."

Millie was glad to see her friend. "I've decided not to live in the hutch anymore," she told him.

"Well, where should we go?"

"I don't know. Let's explore," said Millie happily.

The two rabbits searched until they found a small glade.
There were plenty of flowers to eat and no sign of the
fox. And, by the time summer came, there were lots of
new baby bunnies to keep them company.